THE JOY
OF THE COURT

THE JOY
OF THE COURT

Retold by Constance Hieatt
Illustrated by Pauline Baynes

Thomas Y. Crowell Company   New York

𝔉or 𝔖usie an𝔡 𝔖ally

MANUFACTURED IN THE UNITED STATES OF AMERICA

L.C. Card 73-101931
ISBN 0-690-46572-6
(Library Edition 0-690-46573-4)

1   2   3   4   5   6   7   8   9   10

Preface

The tale of Erec was already a very old story when, around the year 1230, King Haakon of Norway, who loved the stories of King Arthur, asked a writer of his court to translate the French poem *Erec et Enide* into Norwegian. In fact, it is as a whole probably the oldest story of the Arthurian cycle.

Before the end of the twelfth century, there had been a number of versions, agreeing in plot but differing in some details. In France, Chrétien de Troyes had called the hero "Erec," as did Hartmann von Aue in Germany. A Welsh poet called him "Geraint," the name that Tennyson used in his *Idylls of the King* about seven hundred years later.

The only notable change in the story itself over all these centuries was made by Tennyson, who omitted the final episode from which my version takes its title. I follow my medieval predecessors in considering it an integral part of the story, and hope that my readers will agree that it is a very satisfactory ending.

I also hope they will sometimes be amused by my hero: he is just like other people, which means he can be pretty ridiculous at times, though when he is at his best he is a man we can all admire.

Retold by Constance Hieatt

THE JOY OF THE COURT

THE KNIGHT OF THE CART

THE KNIGHT OF THE LION

SIR GAWAIN AND THE GREEN KNIGHT

Contents

1
The Hunt of the
White Stag

Once long ago when it was May in Camelot, King Arthur held a high feast for his court. Kay and Lancelot, Gawain and Ywain, were all there, and many others, including a gay young knight who had but recently come to court. His name was Erec, son of King Erbin of Carnant, and everyone thought him the most promising young man to come to court for many a year. All these knights and their fair ladies were gathered in the hall when, at the height of the merriment, a young lad clad in green, bearing the bow and arrows of a forester, came among them and made his way to the king's throne. He knelt down at Arthur's feet and said, "Hail, my lord, King Arthur!"

"Hail, good youth, and welcome here," replied the king, "whoever you may be. Do you bring tidings to us?"

"You should know me, sire," said the youth, "for I am your own forester in the Forest of Dean. I do indeed bring you tidings. I have seen a great stag in the forest, a stag such as I have never seen before."

"Many and great are the stags in the Forest of Dean," said King Arthur.

"But this one is pure white, lord," the forester replied, "and his antlers are gleaming silver."

"Never have I heard of such a stag," said the king, "but this I know: his appearance must be a sign that a great adventure awaits one of us here. You have done well to tell me this news. Tomorrow I shall hunt the white stag, and all my knights, if they so wish, shall come."

Of course, every knight was eager to join the chase. Queen Guinevere spoke next: "And may not the ladies ride, too, dear lord?'' she asked. ''It would be a shame for us to miss such rare sport.''

''We will be glad of your company,'' said her husband, the king. ''If you will rise before dawn, you may ride with us — but on no account will we wait for any who lag behind!'' Turning to the others, he added, ''Come, friends, let us retire, so that we may rise early to ride after the white stag in the morning. To make you hunt the more eagerly, I declare that he who slays the beast shall award its head to the fairest lady in the court, whoever he deems that to be!''

Many an eager young man slept fitfully that night, for all were impatient for the morning and the great hunt. Each knight hoped to present the prize to his own lady, so that she might be honored as the loveliest of all. Well before dawn they assembled and made ready to ride to the forest with the young forester as their guide. But there was no sign of Queen Guinevere.

''Sire,'' said Sir Gawain to the king, ''shall I go and fetch the queen? It was her wish to ride with us.''

''Wake her not,'' said King Arthur, ''since it seems she would rather sleep than hunt.'' He spurred his horse and rode off, and with him rode the knights of the court, except for young Erec who, like the queen, had kept to his bed too long.

Thus when Guinevere awoke, she found that she had been left behind. Determined not to miss all the fun, she hastily made herself ready and, taking one of her maidens for company, went to the stable herself for horses. There she found she was not quite alone. Erec, too, had just come out, and was mounting his dapple-gray steed. Brightly dressed for the hunt in a coat of

3

flowered silk from Constantinople, a gold-hilted sword at his side, he was a gay escort for a queen, and Guinevere was well pleased to have him riding by her side.

On into the forest they went, listening for the hounds and hunting horns, but there was nothing at all to be heard except the song of the birds in the trees, for the hunt was too far ahead of them. The three companions rode first one way, then another, looking for the tracks of the horses, until at last they heard the sound of hoofs in the wood.

Thinking that they had at last come up with some of their friends, they turned in the direction that the sounds came from. As they drew near, however, they saw that it was not Arthur, or any of his court, but a group of three strangers that rode through the forest. There came first an ugly dwarf, a mean expression on his face, holding a knotted whip in his hand. Some distance behind the dwarf rode a tall knight in full armor, who carried a long, sharp lance. Between the knight and the dwarf rode a damsel on a palfrey. This lady was poorly clad in old, torn garments of plain white linen. Her head hung down in dejection, and her long golden hair hid her face. It seemed quite clear that she rode against her will. Her horse was led by the dwarf, who gave it a lash when it faltered, and spurred by the knight, who prodded it from behind with his spear.

"Erec," said the queen, "do you know who that tall knight is?"

"No, my lady," said Erec, "but I do not think all can be well for the lady who rides so sadly with him."

4

"Go quickly," said Guinevere to the maiden who rode with her, "and bid yonder knight come to me."

The queen's maiden rode straight toward the strange knight, but the dwarf leapt forward into her way, crying, "Halt! You may come no closer."

"Let me pass," said she, "for I bring this knight a message from the queen."

"You may not approach my lord," said the dwarf, blocking the road.

Still she tried to pass him, but the dwarf raised his whip and struck her a cruel blow across the face. Weeping with pain, the maiden made her way back to the queen, who was stricken with grief and anger.

"Ah, Erec," Guinevere cried, "my poor maiden has been cruelly treated! What sort of uncourteous knight is this who would allow his dwarf to so abuse an innocent young girl?"

"I swear I shall avenge that blow," said Erec, turning his horse to ride after the tall knight.

"Oh, stay!" cried Guinevere. "He is armed for battle, and you are not; you have no weapon but a sword, while he has his lance ready, and you have not so much as a shield to protect you."

But Erec would not listen to his queen's counsel. Bidding the ladies farewell, he spurred his horse and left the queen to comfort her maiden alone in the forest.

It was not very much later that Guinevere heard the sound of the hunting horns. The king had slain the great white stag, and the hunt was over. Guinevere rode on, guided by the notes

of the horns, and found her lord King Arthur, gathered with all his knights around the great white stag. Together they rode back to Camelot, bearing the stag's head with its silver antlers. The people lined the streets in great excitement to see that wonderful trophy, and everyone wondered which lady would now be honored by the king's gift.

But at supper that night, the court was not as friendly as usual. Each knight thought his own lady loveliest, and swore that she, and she alone, deserved the honor of the prize. Sir Gawain grew very uneasy. "Sire," he said to his uncle the king, "I fear there is going to be trouble here, for every man wants the white stag's head for his own lady, and no matter whom you award it to, even if it is the queen herself, everyone else will be dissatisfied."

The wise king replied, "God forbid that there should be strife in my court over this. Tell me, good nephew, what do you counsel me to do?"

"Perhaps," said Gawain, "a delay would help tempers to cool off. You could postpone the award until Sir Erec returns, for the hunt cannot be said to be over until all who went forth are back in your hall."

"That is good counsel," said Queen Guinevere, "for there were more adventures today than you know." And she told them what she had seen in the woods: how a tall knight had caused his dwarf to insult the queen and abuse her maiden, and how Erec had ridden off, unarmed as he was, to avenge the injuries done there. "I greatly fear," she added, "that he has acted rashly. He is a strong and brave young knight, but what chance could he have, with only a sword, against a fully-armed knight?"

But just then a steward entered the hall and brought them news: to their gates had come a strange knight, in torn and battered armor, and with him a dwarf.

8

"Is the knight a very tall man, and the dwarf small and ugly?" asked Queen Guinevere.

"Yes, my lady," the steward replied.

"Surely that must be the very same knight we met this morning," said the queen. "I wonder why he has come here. I pray that he has not defeated Sir Erec! And is there a lady with him, clothed in plain white linen?"

"No, madam," said the steward. "He is quite alone except for the dwarf. He has been in a battle recently, for his shield is badly dented, and he is a dreadful sight."

"Bring him in," commanded King Arthur. "We shall soon see just what has happened."

2
Erec's Joy

Into the hall came the tall knight, and with him the dwarf who had so vilely mistreated the queen's maiden. The knight kneeled down before the queen. "Lady," he said, "I bring you greetings from Erec, the boldest and best of knights. I am his prisoner, and he has sent me to you. I bring you my dwarf. He comes to surrender to you, too. We are both at your mercy."

"Since you ask for mercy," said Queen Guinevere, "I shall, for my part, pardon you; I wish no man any harm. But tell us your name, sir knight, and give us news of Erec. Why is he not with you?"

"My name is Yder, son of Nudd," the tall knight replied. "Erec sends you word that he will return tomorrow; he hopes to bring you a pleasant surprise."

This, of course, made everyone the more curious. But they could get no more from Yder, and so they had to rest content with the knowledge that Erec was safe and await his return.

When the next morning was almost past, the watchers on the ramparts saw Erec drawing near, and one of them went to report to the king and queen. "My liege lord and lady," he said, "I think I see Erec approaching. With him there ride three others — a white-haired old man, and an old woman, and a young maiden clothed in white linen. All three are ragged and shabby, but the maiden's hair shines like gold in the sun."

Everyone rose at once, and lost no time gathering by the gate where Erec approached. King Arthur himself came forth to greet him, and lifted the maiden down from her horse. Everyone gasped at her beauty, for despite her threadbare garments she was as lovely a creature as anyone could imagine. Guinevere recognized her as the lady who had ridden the day before in the company of Yder and the dwarf, and the queen stepped forward to greet her and welcome her kindly to the court.

"My lady queen," said Erec, "this is Enid, my bride-to-be. Do not despise her for her humble garments, for she is as noble as she is beautiful. Her father and mother, who come with her, are gentlefolk, kinsmen of dukes and princes, who have fallen through ill luck into poverty. I am giving them a great city to rule in my father's realm, the land of Carnant. It is little enough to give them, for they are giving me their greatest treasure and joy, fair Enid."

Now Guinevere took the ladies off to her chambers where she dressed them in beautiful clothes and rich jewels, and gave orders to her servants to prepare a marriage feast fit for a royal wedding. Meanwhile Erec explained to the king and the knights of the court that Yder had carried Enid off against her will when she refused to marry him; but Erec, angered by the dwarf's treatment of the queen's maiden, had followed and challenged him to battle. In spite of his lack of arms and armor, Erec had defeated Yder and rescued the lady Enid. And when he had seen how lovely she was, Erec wished to win her for himself. She, liking him well, said she would consent if her father gave his blessing.

Thus Erec had sent Yder back to the court, and had taken Enid to her parents, who were overjoyed to see her safe and sound. They gladly consented to the marriage, delighted to see their daughter matched with the brave young son of a rich and powerful king.

Guinevere returned, leading Enid with one hand and Enid's mother with the other. Enid was clothed in embroidered silk, with a coronet of flowers on her bright hair; and her mother wore velvet, all lined with ermine. The mother was handsome and noble to see, the daughter far lovelier than the flowers she wore.

"Fair is your bride, Erec," said the king, "and it is right that she should be, for her mother is a fair and noble lady, and her father a gentle knight. Now I see, too, that Gawain was right when he counseled me not to award the stag's head until your return. It rightly belongs to Enid; surely none can deny that she is the loveliest lady in the court. What say you, my knights?"

In the greatest of good humors, the court agreed that Enid should have the white stag's head. And then it was time to take the bride and groom off to church, where they were married and blessed by the archbishop.

All the bells rang joyously, and a great feast followed. There was singing and dancing and storytelling; musicians played merrily on the harp and the violin, the flute and the pipes; drums and trumpets echoed in the great hall; and no one, rich or poor, was turned away from the doors. Cooks, bakers, and butlers flew about everywhere, providing all the bread and wine and pastries and venison and sweets that any guest could possibly want.

For a full three weeks, the feasting and celebrations went on, but it all mattered little to the newly-wedded pair themselves. They were sufficient joy for each other, and they were so happy together they hardly noticed the time go by at all. But Erec was missed by his friends.

As the weeks passed and the wedding festivities came to an end, the other knights began to miss their gay young friend, who was now so taken up with his bride that he spent little time with anyone else. They rode on hunts, but Erec would not come. Great tournaments were held to which all the champions of

Britain came, but Erec would not join in. And Enid was glad, for she had her knight always by her side.

Then a day came when King Arthur met with the knights of his high council, and they decided that some action should be taken about a matter that had been concerning them. One of their number had long been missing, a good knight called Mabon; after his disappearance, many knights had gone in search of him, but none had ever returned. Arthur thought he knew where the trail ended, and it was determined that the chief knights of the court would set out in search of Mabon and the others who had disappeared. When this decision was reached, Sir Gawain came to call upon Erec, and asked him to join the expedition. But Erec said he would not go.

"Dear friend," said the wise and courteous Gawain, "you cannot mean that. It is a great honor to a young knight that Arthur, most famous of all the kings of earth, should ask him to join in a quest of grave importance."

"Such affairs of state are Arthur's concern, not mine," said Erec. "As for me, I will not leave the side of my sweet fair lady, for here I have found all the joy that a man could ask."

With those words, he turned from Sir Gawain and bent a loving glance at fair Enid, who cast down her lashes and blushed.

But Enid began to wonder if she had done wrong in encouraging Erec to stay always by her side. She was uneasy that Erec rejected Gawain's counsel so, and wondered what his fellow knights would think of him. And it was with reason that she was concerned, for as the days went by, there was much talk about Erec and the words of men reached Enid's ears. She heard them saying that it was a pity so brave a man should turn into a coward for love of a woman, and more and more they said that Erec was now a weakling and no man. This was a great grief to the gentle lady, though she dearly loved her lord and delighted in his company.

And so it was that when Erec and Enid had been married for only a month or two, a night came when the young bride was too unhappy to sleep, and tossed and turned beside her beloved husband.

3
Enid's Grief

As the light of dawn entered their chamber, Enid looked at her sleeping lord, so young and strong and handsome, and she wept bitter tears. "Alas," she cried, "that ever I came here! Wretch that I am, I have brought shame upon him who should have been the best knight in the world. Oh, Erec, miserable are you among men!"

As she spoke in her grief, her tears fell on Erec's face, and he heard her words, for he did not slumber as soundly as she thought. By the time she had spoken her last few words, he was wide awake, wondering what they could mean. "Lady," he said very suddenly, "what is this that you say?"

"Nothing, dear lord," said Enid, wiping her eyes hastily.

"You do not speak the truth, lady," said Erec, "for I heard you, and I see you have been weeping. Surely you do not weep for nothing."

"You are not quite awake," Enid answered, "and cannot see me clearly. Whatever you heard must have been part of a dream."

"Then," said Erec, "it was a dream I do not care to have ever again. It seemed to me that you, my wife, called me miserable and lamented the day that you ever came here with me."

"That is not possible, lord," said Enid. "You know as well as I do the joy we have had with each other."

"Come, wife, this will not do!" cried Erec. "I heard your words, and I know it was no dream. Tell me the truth. If you do not, it will be the worse for you, I swear."

"Then, sir," she said, "since you leave me no choice, I must perforce tell you. I grieve because I hear all men, high and low, say that since you married me you have become a coward and care nothing for the world of men. They say that you were a gallant knight, but by my fault you have become lazy and worthless. This is why I grieve, for I feel it is my fault, and my fault alone, if you have so lost your good reputation."

"Woman," said Erec, "this is quite enough. If you doubt that you have married a brave knight — "

"But I do not doubt it!" cried Enid. "It is only that others say — "

"Silence!" roared Erec. "I have heard quite enough from you. Go from my side at once; put on the linen garments in which you came to the court, and prepare to ride off."

Bitterly weeping, Enid left to do as Erec bade her. "Oh," she wailed, "what a fool I was! Now my beloved lord is going to send me into exile, and I shall never see him again. He was too fond of me, and now I am to be punished, for he will never care for me again."

Half blinded by tears, Enid put on her old, torn clothes, and prepared to mount her palfrey and ride off into exile. But while she was dressing, Erec called for his armor and armed himself well. Then he sent his squire to find his wife, saying, "Tell my lady to come at once; she is keeping me waiting too long."

The squire went quickly, and found Enid all ready, weeping by herself. "My lady," said the squire, "my lord bids you come at once, for he is ready to go."

Greatly astounded, Enid wiped away her tears and quietly followed the squire. "I am quite ready, sir," she said when she came into Erec's presence. "But I know nothing of your thoughts."

"Nor shall you as yet," said Erec shortly, and he bade her mount her steed. "Ride ahead of me," he commanded, "and keep a good lead. Whatever you see or hear, do not turn back, and unless I speak to you, do not dare to say a word to me."

"It shall be as you say, sir," said Enid, and they rode on their way. But it was not a very pleasant way, for Erec chose a wild and dangerous road where there were likely to be thieves and robbers and fierce wild beasts.

Before they had gone very far, a robber knight spied them from the woods. He turned to his two companions and said, "Here is a great chance coming for us! Yonder comes a fair lady guarded by only one knight. Let us take the horses and armor, and the lady, too. I saw them first, and it is my right to deal the first blow."

He rode toward Erec, holding his shield in defensive position, with his two companions following. Enid, seeing them come out of the woods, was stricken with fear. "Lord God," she thought, "what can I do? My lord forbids me to speak to him, but if I hold my tongue he will surely be killed, for there can be no fair contest when three men ride against one! But I should rather die by his hand than fall captive to another; I cannot let him be slain, I must speak."

Turning her horse back, she called to Erec, "Guard yourself, sir. There come riding here three knights, and I fear they will do you harm!"

"Did I not bid you hold your tongue?" said Erec. "You have been bold to disobey me. If it should happen again, it will not be forgiven." Then, taking up his lance, he rushed at the knight

22

who was riding straight at him, and they crashed together so violently that the robber knight flew up in the air and landed on the ground with a crash, too stunned to move for some time.

But his two comrades were hard behind him, and now Erec had two foes to face at once. Turning his horse in a swift circle, he unhorsed the second with a sweep of his lance and made straight for the third, who was now so terrified that he tried to flee. But Erec rode off after him, and in no time at all, all three of the would-be robbers were flat on the ground, begging for mercy.

23

Leaving them there, with many wounds and bruises to remember him by, Erec took their three horses and tied the bridles together. He led them back to the roadside, where Enid was waiting, and bade her to ride on ahead, driving the three horses before her. "And see that you are not so bold as to speak unless you are spoken to. I shall not let you off so easily another time."

"I shall do exactly as you wish, fair sir," Enid replied meekly, and she held her peace as they rode on.

They traveled on through a dark forest, and as they came out of it, they found themselves entering a deep valley. Hiding in a grove at the bottom of the valley were five villainous knights who saw them coming and rejoiced. The first said, "Behold the rich plunder that is coming our way! The damsel is mine — I saw her first!" The second said, "I shall take the black horse."

"The white one will suit me," said the third. "The chestnut is the best of the lot, and that will be my share," said the fourth. The fifth vowed that he would have the horse and armor of the knight himself, and made ready to lead the attack.

But as Enid approached the thicket where the assassins waited, she saw the sunlight gleam on their helmets, and she checked her horse and started back. "My lord, my lord!" she called. "A band of men lie in ambush there, ready to fall upon us. Oh, take care, or they will surely kill you!"

"What, do you dare disobey me again?" said Erec.

"I cannot let you be taken unaware," Enid protested, "for I fear that you will be slain!"

"Silence!" said Erec, as he put up his shield and braced himself for the attack.

The first of the five rushed at him, but Erec thrust with his shield, so that the blow glanced aside, and a second later struck back so hard that the robber knight fell from his horse and broke his leg. The others closed in, but they fared no better. One after another, they fell in the dust, and Erec had gained five more horses.

These five he tied with the other three, and gave all eight to Enid to drive. He commanded her to go along quickly, and not to address him again; and she did not dare say a word in reply, but did as he bade, though it was very hard for her to control all eight horses at once.

And so they rode on, through valleys and plains, and into another great forest when night began to fall.

"Wife," said Erec, "the night is coming, and we can go no further today."

"Indeed, my lord," Enid replied, "I will gladly do whatever you wish."

"Then it is time to rest," he said. "I will watch, if you wish to sleep."

"No, lord," said Enid, "that would not be right; you are the more tired, and it is for you to sleep. I will watch tonight."

Erec agreed to this and, placing his shield under his head, stretched out on the ground. Enid took off her cloak and covered him with it from head to toe. And so he slept the night through, but Enid, holding the reins of the horses, stood and watched all night, silently mourning and lamenting the day she had been so unwise as to anger her lord.

"Alas," she said, "that ever I could have said that men thought him a coward — he who thinks nothing of fighting three or five men at once! And I, poor wretch that I am, may not even speak to my lord without making him angry. Oh, what is to become of us? This is an evil and dangerous road, and he cannot go on like this forever, fighting against worse and worse odds!"

4
The Treachery of
Count Galan

Thus Enid lamented the whole night through, but when morning came and Erec awoke, she dried her eyes and turned a meek and humble face to hear what his wishes might be.

"Take the horses," said Erec, "and lead the way. Keep your distance, and do not dare to look back at me or speak out of turn again."

And so they went forward once more, Enid in front with eight horses to drive, and Erec some lengths behind. After a while, they arrived at the edge of the forest, and found themselves on a great open plain where meadows ran down to a town not far ahead. Men with scythes were mowing the hay in the meadows. A river ran through the plain, and they made their way toward it, for they were very thirsty and the horses had need of water. A road ran along the river's edge; along it was riding a squire and two servants, bearing bread and cheese and beer for the mowers. When they saw Erec and Enid, coming from the direction of the forest, they were much surprised, for they knew there was no town or dwelling for a day's ride in that direction.

Quickly the squire rode forward. "Good sir knight, I see that you come from the forest, where you can have had no pleasant night's rest, nor can you have found much to eat or drink. I have food here to bring to the mowers; it is simple fare, but I would be honored if you and your lady would accept it from us."

"I will," said Erec, "and may God repay you."

He dismounted from his horse, while the squire helped Enid to the ground. They made a hearty breakfast, for they had long gone without any food.

When they had eaten their fill, Erec said, "Friend, as a

reward, I pray you take one of these horses; they are all I have to offer you. Take any one that you like."

"I ask no reward, sir," said the squire, "and that which you offer is far greater than I could deserve."

"But you may earn it, if you will," Erec replied. "For if it were not a hardship for you, I would be glad if you would ride to the nearest town and find lodging for us there."

The squire agreed to do this, and sending the servants on to the mowers with the rest of the food and drink, he chose a fine chestnut horse and rode to the town where he engaged rooms and quickly returned to lead Erec and Enid back. There they were greeted courteously. Good provision was made for their horses, and they were led into a spacious and comfortable chamber where the squire bade them farewell and left them to take their rest.

Mounting his new horse, the squire rode to the stables of his lord, Count Galan, the ruler of that town. As he rode up, the count, seeing his squire mounted upon the fine horse, asked him whose horse that might be.

"It is mine, my lord," said the squire, and told him how he had found a strange knight coming out of the forest, who had given him one of his horses in gratitude for his provision of food and lodgings. "He seems a most noble knight," he added, "and with him is a lady so fair that I have never seen a lady half so fair as she."

Now the count was very curious to see the strange knight and his lady, and when Erec and Enid had had time to rest, he went to their lodgings to call upon them.

There he was received very courteously by Erec, but saw no sign of the lady, until looking about more closely, he saw where she sat by herself, at the far end of the room. He wondered why she seemed to be banished from the company of the knight, but he was too courteous to ask questions about the matter. He asked only that Erec tell him, if he would, where he rode and on what errand.

"I ride only where I please," Erec answered, "seeking adventures on my way."

Count Galan had to be satisfied with that answer, and they spoke for a while of many things, until at last the count asked if he might be allowed to speak with the lady he saw at the end of the room.

"I have no objection," said Erec.

The count moved down to the corner where Enid sat, and he marveled at her great beauty. He wondered at her poor and ragged attire and timid manner, and thought it a shame to find her here when she would have graced the most splendid court.

"Lady," he said, "it is not right for so fair a creature as you to wander about in such hardship, with no one to guard and care for you but a knight who treats you with scant courtesy."

"He is my lord and husband," said Enid. "My place is by his side. Whether in forest or castle, that is for him to decide."

"Sweet lady, you deserve a better lord, who values you as he ought," the count replied. "Stay here with me, and I shall make you lady over all my lands; nevermore shall you lack rich robes, servants, and every comfort. I swear I will serve and honor you all the days of my life."

32

"You do wrong to ask me to break my faith," Enid replied indignantly. "I shall never agree to desert my dear lord."

"These are foolish words," said Count Galan, flushing with sudden anger. "I warn you of one thing: you are in my land, and I have power here to do as I wish. If you will not stay with me of your own free will, then I can kill your knight and force you to do as I say."

He started to draw his sword. Enid, fearing that he would slay Erec on the spot, reached out her hand to detain him and spoke quickly: "Do not be so hasty, good sir," she said, "for I spoke but to test your love for me. I will gladly do as you say, for I am weary of this hard life. But if you attack him now, you will put yourself in great danger, for he thinks nothing of fighting three or more men at once. Wait until morning; then you can bring help with you, and catch him as he prepares to leave. It will be better so."

Satisfied with this reply, Count Galan took his leave. Erec soon turned to his rest, knowing nothing of what had been said — for he forbade Enid to speak to him. He slept soundly enough, but Enid watched through the night again in terror lest the count should return. If she did not warn Erec, he would surely be captured by the count's men in the morning; but she hesitated to anger him by breaking his command once again. At last, though, her fear became too strong, and she made up her mind to disobey.

"Awake, lord Erec," she said. "Oh, pardon me, but I must speak before we are both lost. The count is a traitor; he would have killed you this night if I had not said I would be his wife. Soon now he will return with all his men, and you will be trapped here if you are inside. Oh, hurry, so that we can make our escape while there is still time!"

Erec rose at once, and this time he did not take Enid to task for speaking out of turn. "Lady," he said, "run and see that our horses are saddled, and send our host to me while I arm."

When the host came up, astounded that his guests were eager to depart although it was not yet day, Erec asked him to take the seven horses in payment for his expenses.

"But you do not owe me a quarter as much as the value of those horses," said the host in amazement.

"Nonetheless, they are all yours," said Erec.

The host bowed low, too speechless to thank him in words,

but Erec did not wait to hear any. He was ready to mount his horse, and quickly he made his farewells and rode off, bidding Enid to ride behind.

Only a few minutes after they left, the count came with a hundred knights, and surrounded the house where he thought he would find Erec and Enid. When he discovered that the lady had deceived him, he was very angry indeed, and began to search for the tracks of the horses, vowing that he would have no mercy if he came up with the fugitives. Finding the trail, he rode on with his hundred knights until they caught a glimpse of two horses and riders ahead by the edge of a wood. Then they spurred their steeds harder yet, and the dust flew from their horses' hoofs.

Enid looked back about then, and saw what seemed to be a great cloud moving quickly toward them. From that cloud she heard the clang of armor and the pounding of hundreds of hoofs, and she saw that a great host bore down upon them. "Erec!" she cried. "Fly into the wood! The count is upon us, and with him a great host of armed knights!"

But, instead of fleeing into the safety of the forest, Erec stopped at once and turned his horse back. "Never shall I flee from open battle," he said, "for I am no coward, whatever you may think."

"Oh, my dear lord," Enid cried, "it is madness to stay in this plain, for no man is a match for an army!"

"Go you and take refuge, if you wish," said Erec. "As for me, I will not move from this spot."

5
Erec's Way

As the first few of Count Galan's knights rode up, Erec lunged at each, and with the first thrust of his lance swept them off their horses, one by one, until he was surrounded by so many that he could no longer deal with them one at a time. But at that moment the count himself came forward and ordered his men to move back, for he wished to fight Erec in single combat because of the grudge he bore. Now the count was a strong and courageous knight who put such trust in his own strength and skill that he had come with no arms but a lance and a spear, thinking he needed no more. In this he was ill advised, for Erec was no ordinary opponent.

The two knights came together with such violence that the count's spear broke on Erec's shield, which cracked in two. But Erec then ran his spear through the count's shield, knocking him senseless from his steed. The count's men then spurred their horses and rode forward, all closing in on Erec at once, so that it was hardly possible for him to protect himself and his shield was now all but useless. But the wounded count drew himself up and called out to his men, ordering them to stop. "Hold and turn back," he cried, "for I repent what I have done. I deserve this for my treachery."

Reluctantly his men backed off, and came to minister to him where he lay sorely wounded. But Erec did not stop to discuss the matter; although he was wounded himself, he turned and rode off at full speed into the forest with Enid behind him.

And so they rode all morning until they came to a bridge over a river, leading to a high walled town; a knight stood guard over the bridge. Erec turned to cross the river, but the knight challenged him and said, "This road is forbidden."

"Who dares to tell me what road I may take?" asked Erec.

"The lord of this land, King Guivret the Little, allows no one here without his permission," answered the knight. "It is most likely that you will earn nothing but shame if you try to defy him."

"I shall do just as I please despite him," said Erec and started across the bridge. The guard made no move to stop him, so Enid followed along behind. The road from here wound uphill, but as they were mounting that hill, a knight came racing down from the gates of the city. He was small in stature, but well armed, and mounted on a powerful steed, which came at such a pace that it crushed the stones beneath its hoofs, so that sparks flew in all directions and it was as if the steed's four feet were on fire. Enid drew up and stayed stock-still while Eric held sword and lance before him, braced for attack.

But when the knight came up to them, he halted abruptly, and his horse danced in place as he called, "What do you do here, sir knight? Do you come in ill will, to challenge me?"

"Not so," said Erec. "I wish only to go my way in peace."

"It is forbidden for strangers to pass this way," said the knight. "But I see you have been in battle, and I have no wish to take advantage of a man who is already weakened by wounds. I am the king of this place, and I shall forgive you if you will come to my court so that my people can attend to your wounds."

"I will not come to any man's court," said Erec. "Let me pass."

"Sir knight, you speak discourteously," said the king much

displeased. "You shall accept my hospitality or my enmity — one or the other."

"Then let it be enmity," said Erec defiantly.

Now both knights were very angry, and they set upon each other, and dealt each other blow after blow, until both their horses were brought to their knees and they had to continue the fight on foot.

Erec was astonished at the small king's nimbleness — he always seemed to be out of the way of each blow. But the fight was fierce on both sides. Each of them slashed the other's armor until it hung in shreds, but neither was willing to stop though it looked as if it would end in both of them being killed. Enid was beside herself with grief, but nothing would make them cease. Still they fought on, knocking the jewels from each other's helmets and dealing out terrible wounds.

At last, though, the little king dealt Erec such a blow that he staggered and almost fell to the ground, but the sword broke off at the hilt in Erec's shield, so that it was now useless. Seeing this, King Guivret threw away the remains of his sword and cried out to Erec for mercy. "I yield to you, sir knight," he cried, "for now I have lost my sword and cannot defend myself."

"I will grant that, then," said Erec and put aside his sword.

"Then also grant me leave to have your wounds seen to," said Guivret the Little. "We both have need of a physician, and I assure you, sir, that all in my court will do you honor."

"Nevertheless," said Erec, "I shall not come. I ask of you only one thing — that if you should hear I have need of aid, you will not forget me."

"I promise you that, and gladly," said Guivret; and the two knights were as great friends as they had been bitter enemies not long since. Each cut off strips from his own shirt and bound the other's wounds, and when they had bandaged each other, they embraced and took their leave with vows of eternal friendship.

Guivret was uneasy, however, to see Erec ride on in such condition, for he saw he was hardly able to stay on his horse. And Enid, glad as she was that Erec was still alive after all, grieved that he would not have his wounds tended, and rode behind him, watching him anxiously lest he should faint or fall.

Now as they rode through a valley, the heat of the day was great, and Erec's broken armor was sticking to his flesh and giving him much discomfort. Finally he halted under a tree to rest, and as they rested there, they heard horns close at hand, and knew that men were mustered in a camp nearby. This, though Erec did not then know it, was King Arthur with the best knights of his court, riding on their quest. As Erec was wondering which way he should go to avoid the encampment, he realized it was too late: a knight had already caught sight of him and was riding up rapidly.

This was Sir Kay; but he did not recognize Erec, for Erec was stained with blood and dirt, and his arms were battered beyond all recognition. Enid, seeing that Erec did not wish to be known, drew her cloak over her face and shrank back into the shadows.

"What are you doing here, knight?" asked Kay.

"I am resting in the shade of a tree, avoiding the heat of the sun," said Erec.

"Who are you, and what journey are you on?" asked Kay.

"I shall not tell you that," replied Erec.

"Be not angry," said Kay. "I ask it for your own good. I see that you are wounded and hurt. Come with me to my lord King Arthur, and you shall be well cared for."

"I will not," said Erec. "Let me be, for I must go on my way while there is still daylight."

"If you will not take my advice, you shall be made to come," said Kay, and he stepped forward and grabbed the bridle of Erec's horse. Angered, Erec struck him with the butt of his spear, so that he fell to the ground. Now Kay was stricken with fear, and he quickly remounted his horse and rode back to the camp where he went straight to Sir Gawain.

"Lord Gawain," he said, "I have just now heard that there is a wounded knight in the forest. It would be fitting if you would go and bring him back here"; for Kay did not like to admit that he had run from a man so sorely wounded that he could scarcely sit on his horse.

And so Gawain went to Erec, but Erec would not go with him either. The two were closing in for a fight when suddenly Gawain recognized Erec and called a halt to the battle. Quickly Gawain hailed a squire who stood nearby and told him to fetch the king at once, and he held Erec in conversation so long that, whether Erec liked it or not, it became too late for him to go on that day. Meanwhile Arthur came with a tent and had it pitched by the tree where Erec stood.

Then, at last, Erec had to give in and accept the hospitality of the court, which much cheered Enid.

As Arthur lifted her to the ground, he said, "Alas, dear lady, what journey is this?"

"I know not, sire," said she, "save that it pleases my husband."

"Surely he is riding to his death," said the king, "unless he will accept our counsel and stay with us until his wounds are healed."

But Erec would not hear of any such thing. It was with a bad grace that he accepted lodging for the night, and allowed the king's physicians to treat his wounds with a precious ointment made by Morgan le Fay. But on no account would he agree to stay longer than one night.

"To leave as you are now, far from well, would be a great

mistake," said King Arthur. "It would cause us all great grief if you were to die on your journey. We beg of you, remain with us for a week at least, to give your wounds time to mend."

But it was no use. Early next morning, Erec ordered the horses saddled, and armed himself to ride. All the knights gathered around and tried to persuade him to stay, but he would not listen. With Enid riding behind, he departed. None there thought that they would ever see him again.

"I grieve for the good lady," said Gawain, "for her lord leads her into danger."

"He lacks counsel," agreed King Arthur.

"He is altogether too fond of having his own way," said Kay.

But Arthur replied, "And are you not fond of yours, Kay?"

6
The Brief
Widowhood of Enid

Erec and Enid followed the road for some distance, until as they passed through a wood, they heard a terrible shrieking close by.

"Stay here," said Erec, "and wait for me while I find what this outcry may mean."

He rode into a clearing in the wood where he found a damsel wailing and tearing her hair and her garments. Erec, in great wonder, begged her to tell him why she cried out so, and at last she spoke to him. "Alas, fair sir," the damsel said, "woe is me, for my knight has been captured by two cruel giants, and they will surely slay him!"

"Which way did they go?" asked Erec.

"That way, my lord, along the road. But there is no use in following them, for each one is bigger than two tall men, and they would surely capture you, too."

But Erec said that nonetheless he would free her knight or die in the attempt. He led her back to the roadside where Enid waited, and told them to stay there together to await his return.

Spurring his horse, he followed the trail of the giants until

he caught sight of them ahead on the road. The two giants bore neither shields nor swords, but both had huge clubs, tipped with iron, with which they beat the helpless knight bound to his horse between them.

"Hold!" cried Erec wrathfully. "Churls, how dare you mistreat a good knight so?"

The giants turned and threatened Erec with their clubs. "It is no business of yours," one replied; and the other said, "Get out of our sight, or you shall be heartily sorry."

Erec paid no heed to their threats, but rode straight at them and ran the first through with his spear. But at the same moment the second giant struck him so hard with his club that Erec's wounds opened and he was bathed in blood. Still, he was able to draw his sword, and he dealt the giant such a blow that the huge man fell to the ground with a crash like a falling tree; neither of the two wicked giants would trouble the world again.

Then Erec turned to the captive knight and freed him; and the knight wept for joy, saying, "Good sir, I owe you my life. How can I ever repay you? Let me ride with you and serve you as my lord."

"I do not wish that," said Erec. "But there is one who waits anxiously for you. I found your good lady sorrowing in the wood. Let us return together to comfort her with the news that you are safe."

"Will you not tell me your name and country, so that I may seek you and serve you?" asked the knight.

"No," said Erec, "but if you wish to know, go and find King Arthur, who is camped with his court a few hours' ride down this road. He will tell you who I am."

The knight was content with this and rode back with Erec to the place where the two ladies waited, trembling with fear lest both their knights had been killed by the giants. Great was their joy when they saw them return.

The rescued knight, reunited with his lady, now rode off to seek Arthur, saying, "If ever you need my assistance, I am called Cadoc of Tabriol, and I will always be at your service."

They left Erec alone with Enid, who was so relieved to see

her lord return safely that in her joy she did not notice how pale and weak he was. She could not know the pain that he was suffering. Thus it came as a very great shock when Erec suddenly swayed and fell over on his horse's neck. As he tried to straighten up, he slipped out of his saddle and stirrups, and fell to the ground where he lay as if lifeless. Enid gave a terrible shriek and rushed to his side. She knelt and held his head in her lap, calling his name and rubbing his wrists and temples. But he did not revive.

Sobbing, she pulled out Erec's sword and said, "Now that my lord is dead, I do not wish to live; it is through my fault he is slain, for if I had not spoken those fatal words to him, he would never have risked his life so." And she would have killed herself at once, but at this moment a troop of knights rode up. The leader reached out quickly and pulled the sword from her hand, returning it to its sheath.

"Lady," he said, "what has happened here? I am the Duke of Limors, in which land you are. I heard your cries and came to find what is the matter."

"Alas, good sir, I wish to die!" cried Enid. "Here lies dead my lord and my husband, the best knight in the world."

"Who has slain him?" asked the duke.

"He fought with some giants a while ago and slew them both; but the blows they dealt him have been too much, for he was already weakened by wounds from many battles," said Enid, and she wailed and tore her clothes.

"Lady," said the duke, "much mourning will not bring a man back to life. Be wise, and comfort yourself, for you may yet have good fortune. You are very beautiful, and I will gladly make you my wife; you will be a duchess, and with me rule all this land. Be of good cheer!"

"Never!" said Enid. "For God's sake, let me be!"

"Surely you will not refuse to let me take away his body and treat it with due honor?" the duke requested. And though Enid made no reply, he ordered his men to take up Erec's body on a bier and carry it to his castle.

Quickly the men cut down two saplings, and bound branches across it, and on this bier carried off the fallen knight; and Enid followed alongside, never ceasing to weep and lament.

When Erec was laid out in the hall, with his lance and his shield by his side, the duke ordered a great funeral feast — but that was not all, for he fully intended to make it a wedding feast, too. To Enid who mourned by the side of her lord, he said, "Now come away and take food and drink, for the feast is prepared."

54

But Enid swore that no morsel would ever pass her lips again until she could dine with her lord, who lay on the bier. "Lady," said the duke, "you know that can never be. You are talking great nonsense; you must come, and come at once."

"I will not," said Enid.

"I say that you shall," said the duke, and laid hands on her to carry her off to the table by force.

But his knights were alarmed, and one cried, "Stop, sir! This is uncourteous. If the lady is grieved by the death of her lord, no one can say she is wrong."

"Hold your peace," said the duke. "The lady is mine, and I shall do as I please with her, for I intend to make her my wife."

"I will never be wife to any man but him who lies on this bier," cried Enid, and she wailed louder than ever. In his anger, the duke struck her on the face, and she gave out a piercing shriek. "Oh, Erec," she cried, "if you were alive, you would not let any man treat me so!"

And with the echo of that cry, Erec stirred and sat bolt upright. And as he slowly arose from the bier, all the duke's men were frozen with horror to see the corpse come to life.

7
Guivret's Counsel

Erec, of course, had not been dead at all, but only in a deep swoon. The duke's knights did not know that, however. They thought that they saw the dead rise. Hearing Enid's cries and seeing her in the duke's grasp, Erec headed straight for the duke and gave him a mighty blow that toppled him to the floor.

Released from the grasp of her captor, Enid quickly picked up Erec's lance while he grasped his sword and shield. Together they faced the room, but all gave way before them, saying, "Fly, fly — the dead walk, and we shall surely be slain!" Young and old struggled to leave the room as fast as they could, overturning the tables in their haste to flee from the walking corpse. Thus Erec and Enid had no difficulty making their way to the courtyard.

There they found a stable boy leading a horse. He, too, was overcome with terror at the sight of the man whose body had lain on the bier, and he dropped the horse's reins and ran for his life.

This suited Erec well. He grabbed the bridle and mounted the horse. He raised Enid from the ground and placed her before him on the saddle bow, saying, "Dear lady, dearest of friends, forgive me for the way I have treated you. From now on, I promise to do all in my power to serve you as you deserve."

Before she could make any reply, he spurred the horse, and they rode off out of the town as fast as the horse could go. And as they rode through the night, they heard a clatter of horses, and when they looked ahead, they could see spearshafts shining in the moonlight.

"I hear the clamor of a host of men," said Erec. "Quick,

now, hide yourself behind this hedge." And he lifted her down and hid her behind the bushes while he faced the troop that bore down upon him.

But Erec was at the end of his strength. When the knight at the head of the troop rode at him, Erec fell to the earth at once.

Then Enid sprang out from behind the hedge, crying, "Sir, you will gain no glory from slaying a weak and exhausted man! For the love of God, cease this battle!"

"Alas," said the knight, recognizing Enid, "and is this Erec?"

"That it is," the lady replied. "And who are you?"

"I am Guivret the Little," said the knight, jumping down from his horse, "and I was riding to come to your aid." He knelt down by Erec's side, saying, "Forgive me if I have hurt you, my friend. I had heard that the Duke of Limors had carried you off, gravely wounded, and intended to marry your lady. I wished to deliver her and to see if you were indeed dead. Alas, that you would not accept my counsel and be healed of your wounds, so that this misfortune would not have come upon us!"

"I do not blame you, my friend, for you did not recognize me," said Erec. "If you have counsel for me now, I will gladly accept it."

"Then, sir," said Guivret, "I counsel that you come to a castle I have nearby where my sisters will care for you and cure your wounds, for they are skilled in that art."

Erec agreed at once, and they all rode off to the castle where the king's sisters dwelled. There they stayed for several weeks while Erec rested and was cared for by the two sisters, who knew all there was to be known about the art of healing. Guivret had Erec's armor repaired so that it was as good as new, and provided both Erec and Enid with splendid new clothes, for all that they had been wearing was now in shreds.

When the three friends had stayed at the castle for about a month, and Erec was well recovered, they sat together in the garden one day and spoke of various matters. Guivret said that he had heard that Arthur and his knights were riding about the land, and he wondered what their errand might be. "I can tell you that," said Erec, and he sighed for shame that he had not ridden with them. "They search for a knight who has disappeared, and for those who went before to seek him but who have also disappeared."

Guivret pondered this for a while. Finally he said, "Perhaps I could tell them where to look."

"Then tell me, my friend," said Erec eagerly. "I would give all the world if I could now help my good lord King Arthur! I fear that he cannot think well of me, for I refused to join in the quest."

"Sir," said Guivret, greatly distressed, "I would be much better pleased if you did not ask, for the place I know of is perilous. You have risked your life enough; for your lady's sake, do not attempt this dangerous quest."

But Enid said that for her part, she would never wish to hold her lord back from that which he thought it right to do. At last, Guivret gave in and said, "There is a town some leagues from here which is called Brandigan. Men say that there is a perilous adventure there. I know that for more than seven years, no one who has gone to that town in search of adventure has ever returned, yet bold knights have come there from many a land."

"What is the adventure called?" asked Erec.

"It is called 'The Joy of the Court,'" answered Guivret.

"Splendid!" said Erec. "There can be nothing but good in that. I vow I shall go in search of this Joy."

"The name is fair, but none who seek the Joy have returned alive," said Guivret. "If you must needs go, I shall ride with you. Surely you will not refuse my company?"

Erec agreed to his request, and Enid, too, begged to ride with them. Thus the three set out together in the morning, and rode until they came to a place where two roads forked. There Guivret was not quite sure of the way, and when a man on foot came along, they hailed him and asked which road they should take to Brandigan.

"The road to the left goes to Brandigan," said the countryman. "But, sir, it is not a good road to follow. "It would be much better for you to take the road to the right and forget the name of Brandigan."

"I thank you, friend," said Erec, "but that is where I must needs go."

"Alas, sir," the man replied, "then you will have need of God's help. I see that you seek for the Joy of the Court; but all who have looked for that Joy have found it their ruin."

Erec still kept to the road on the left, and with him rode Guivret and Enid. They rode to the end of a valley, where they saw a fine walled town rise before them, and all three went on through the gates of the town.

As they passed through the streets, the townsmen came out and watched, but no one said a word. Erec knew that their silence was caused by fear and pity, and he bowed to the men and women as he passed. Silently they greeted him, and with sad faces watched him ride on until he came to a very strange garden. Then Erec stopped, and spoke to the townspeople watching: "Is the Joy of the Court to be found in this garden?" he asked.

The crowd seemed to hold its breath. At last a young maiden spoke up and said, "Sir, men say it is so, but we fear that this Joy has brought woe to many brave knights. Do not go into the garden, my lord, for you will never come out again."

"What is to keep me there?" asked Erec. "I see no walls or gates."

"Do you not see the mist that surrounds the garden?" replied the maiden. "Any man can pass through that wall of mist, but it never parts to allow one inside to come out."

"I shall see about that," said Erec.

"Look about you," said the young maiden. "Do you not see the helmets and shields of many knights on stakes around the garden? Every one of those belonged to a good knight who passed through the mist. The next day his arms were always found on a stake outside the garden, but not one of the knights has ever come out to claim them. If you enter there, sir knight, your own arms shall appear on such a stake, and you will be as good as dead."

"I have already risen from death once," said Erec. "Perhaps I can return again." He placed Enid's hand in Guivret's, bidding his friend look after his wife, and rode forward into the garden. The mist parted just a little as he went through, then closed and appeared to grow deeper than ever.

8
The Joy of the Court

As Erec rode into the enchanted garden, he saw much that astonished him. In this garden there was no change of season, for each tree bore fruit and flowers and leaves all at the same time. There was no bird on earth that did not sing there, and the sound of the song was an enchantment in itself. Cool streams ran through the garden, and fountains played there; small beasts romped through the grass, quite unafraid. It seemed to be a paradise on earth.

But under the shady trees around the edge of the garden, there were couches covered with silken cushions, and on each couch lay a knight fast asleep. No arms were to be seen, and Erec thought it likely that these were the knights whose shields and helmets were found on the outside of the garden. Still, they certainly did not seem to be dead, but rather, smiling in their sleep as if they were having pleasant dreams.

Leaving them behind, Erec rode straight into the center of the garden, and there he found two golden seats placed under a tree laden with flowers and fruit of all kinds. In one of the golden seats sat a damsel as fair as any lady in the world. She smiled at Erec, and offered him the golden seat beside her. She held in her hand a goblet full of wine from which she begged him to drink, and there were cakes on a salver by her side.

But Erec did not dismount, nor did he accept the cup or the cakes that the damsel held out to him. Instead he looked about him carefully and saw, on a branch of the tree over her head, a silver horn hanging; he reached out to grasp this horn. The damsel cried out in dismay, and at once a knight, clad in red armor, riding on a great charger, came thundering into the center

66

of the garden, crying, "Hold, villain! How dare you touch my horn?"

"Who are you to stop me?" Erec replied.

"I am lord of this garden, and since you challenge me, you must defend yourself well," said the knight. He leveled his lance at Erec, who raised his shield and prepared for battle.

Now both charged furiously at the other, but both lances broke at the first rush, and they had to dismount and continue the fight on foot. Blow after blow was exchanged until neither could see very well and both let their shields fall to the ground. Now they grappled with each other, and each tried to pull the other down to the ground. Thus they fought bitterly for many an hour until finally Erec pinned down his opponent, so that he could not rise again.

"Mercy!" the knight cried. "You have beaten me. I will do whatever you wish."

"Then tell me," said Erec, "how to raise the spell that protects this garden and release the knights that lie sleeping here."

"Then raise the silver horn," said the defeated knight, "and blow it, as you wished to do. When it sounds, the mist will disappear, and all the knights who sleep here will arise."

At once Erec reached for the horn and blew a great blast. The lady who sat in the golden seat gave a great cry and buried her head in her hands; but at that moment all the mist vanished away, and all the sleeping knights stirred on their silken couches and began to awaken from their long rest.

"Now tell me, sir knight," said Erec, "who you are and what has happened here."

"I am called Mabon," said the knight, and before he could continue, Erec exclaimed, "But you are he for whom we search!"

"That is likely enough, I fear," said Mabon, "and in truth I am glad you have found me. Let me tell you how I came to stay in this garden.

"Many years ago," he said, "when I was so young I was hardly more than a child, I made a vow to my sweetheart — the damsel who sits yonder in the golden chair under the tree. I was so fond of her that when she asked me to prove it by promising I would give her any wish she should have were it in my power, I gladly agreed. But her wish was this: that I run away with her and stay forever in this garden, alone with her, never faring forth into the world of men. For her sake, I have done this, and never would I have been released from the vow unless one had come who could break the spell, as you have now done. Others have come before you, but all were captured by the spell of the garden, and only now may they wake again."

By now the other knights were on their feet, though somewhat dazed after their long sleep. Enid and Guivret had ridden in, seeing that the spell had been lifted. All were joyous, except for the lady in the center of the garden who now wept bitterly in fear that her knight would leave her forever.

Seeing this, Enid went to her side and asked her what her trouble was. The lady told her her story, and Enid comforted her as best she could. At length, the two ladies discovered that they were cousins, and had great joy to see each other again, for they had not met since they were young children. And now the lady of the garden asked Enid how she came to be there.

"Fair cousin," said Enid, "I ride with my wedded husband, he who married me with the consent of my father and mother. For a while, like you, we wished to retire from the life of men; but that did not turn out well. For you, too, it may be better to come from this garden now, and join your knight openly in the world outside the garden. Come and see, dear cousin!"

Thus Enid led out the lady of the garden, and as they came outside, they found that Arthur and his knights had just arrived at the town. All were astonished to find Erec there — victorious now, and a hero. In their delight at seeing Mabon again, together with many other good knights, it was long before they had time to ask how all this had come about.

That night Arthur's court, though far from home, held a great feast, camped in a field on the edge of the town of Brandigan. The citizens of the town gladly brought them food and wine of all sorts, including even fruits from the enchanted garden, which were far more delicious than any other fruits on earth. They all wished Mabon to become the lawful lord of the town, and then and there he married his lady, Enid's cousin, and they became the rulers of Brandigan. From then on, the good men of Brandigan welcomed strangers to their city with joy, rather than sorrowful silence; young and old of the town visited the enchanted garden, coming and going as they pleased. The Joy of the Court was now truly a joy to all who came to it.

As for Erec and Enid, they returned to Camelot with King Arthur and spent many happy years at the court, where Erec was one of the king's most trusted knights whenever help or counsel was needed. In later years, word came that Erec's old father, King Erbin, had died, and Erec became king of Carnant. Erec and Enid were crowned king and queen at a great coronation at Christmas time. Guivret the Little came to the coronation, and so did Cadoc of Tabriol, and Mabon, and all the knights who had been delivered when Erec blew the horn and lifted the mist which had bound them.

And, of course, King Arthur came, with Queen Guinevere, and Gawain, and Kay, and all the rest of his court. For Erec was honored far and wide as a brave knight and a good king, of whom it was never again said that he lacked counsel. And Enid, his wife, was his dearest friend and honored lady, who ruled beside him wisely and well for the rest of their long lives together.

About the Author

As a medieval scholar, Constance Hieatt has especially enjoyed retelling Arthurian legends for young readers. THE JOY OF THE COURT is a companion volume to her earlier books: *Sir Gawain and the Green Knight, The Knight of the Lion,* and *The Knight of the Cart.* Mrs. Hieatt is a specialist in Old and Middle English, and the author of several texts, translations, and scholarly commentaries. She has taught at Queensborough Community College and at St. John's University in New York, and is now professor of English at the University of Western Ontario in London, Ontario.

Mrs. Hieatt was born in Boston, Massachusetts, and attended Smith College. She received her A.B. and A.M. degrees from Hunter College, and her Ph.D. from Yale University. She and her husband, who is also a professor of English, spend much of their time in England, where their home is part of a remodeled manor house in a village near Oxford.

About the Illustrator

Pauline Baynes, illustrator of over sixty books, lives with her husband in a small quiet cottage in the English countryside. Miss Baynes has always loved history, and she is especially interested in the medieval period, when she says, "All the best things were built, painted, achieved." She therefore very much enjoyed illustrating Mrs. Hieatt's book.

But there was more than interest and pleasure that qualified Miss Baynes to illustrate THE JOY OF THE COURT. Among the books she had recently illustrated is *A Dictionary of Chivalry* by Grant Uden. In doing that work, she studied even the smallest details of medieval costume and jewelry, and for it she later received England's Kate Greenaway medal for the most distinguished work in the illustration of children's books.